THE PUPPY PLACE

BEAR

ELLEN MILES

D1051802

APPLE

SCHOLASTIC INC.

New York   Toronto   London   Auckland
Sydney   Mexico City   New Delhi   Hong Kong

For Wayne, who loves winter (and dogs) as much as I do.

ISBN-13: 978-0-545-08348-5
ISBN-10: 0-545-08348-6

Cover art by Tim O'Brien
Original cover design by Steve Scott

15 14   12 13 14/0

Printed in the U.S.A.

This edition first printing, September 2009

CHAPTER ONE

"Look — look — look!" The Bean was pointing and shouting. "*B!* I see a *B! B* is for Bean!"

Lizzie had to smile. Her little brother was getting really good at his letters. He could always spot *A* for Adam (his real name, not that anyone ever called him that), *B* for Bean, *C* for Charles (Lizzie's middle brother), and, of course, *L* for Lizzie, who was the oldest. "That's good!" she said, noting that the car passing them also had a *D* and a *Y* in its license plate. Excellent! The Bean wasn't so good at those letters yet, but Lizzie needed both of them for her bingo card.

The Petersons were piled into the family van, and they were driving north. Lizzie liked the sound of that: It was adventurous, like an

1

expedition. So what if they weren't going all the way to the North Pole, or even as far north as Canada? "Will there still be snow, even though it's March?" she had asked when she first heard they were going to Vermont. Lizzie loved being outside, even in winter. *Especially* in winter! She loved sledding, building snow forts and snow-men, and even helping Dad shovel the driveway. The only thing she wasn't so sure about was whether she would enjoy cross-country skiing as much as Dad thought she would.

Lizzie had gone to a ski resort once with her best friend, Maria, and Maria's father. She had been scared of riding the chairlift, a million miles above the snowy hill. She had worried about get-ting *off* the chairlift (how exactly did that work?). And she had been *terrified* of zooming downhill on the two planks that felt stapled to her feet.

Lizzie was strong. She could do twenty pull-ups and she could run fast, but sports that took a lot of coordination were not exactly her specialty.

Thankfully, Mom and Dad said that the resort type of skiing was way too expensive for a family vacation. And Dad kept telling her that cross-country skiing was a lot less scary. "It's just like you're walking through the woods, only on skis," he said again now, as they drove north.

That sounded easier — but it also sounded like a lot of work, trudging through the deep snow. Oh, well. Lizzie was willing to give it a try.

Dad also kept promising that there would be lots of snow in Vermont. "In fact, I heard they had a big snowstorm last week, and there might be another while we're there!" He sounded excited.

"Snow? Where?" The Bean stared out the window.

Lizzie looked too, hoping to see snow on the ground. But all she saw were rocks and dead-looking grass. "We still have two hours to go!" she told her brother. The Bean groaned, but Lizzie didn't mind. She actually liked car trips, the longer the better.

She liked to watch out the window. She liked the special snacks Mom packed, like cheesy crackers and baby carrots. And she liked how her family played games like Twenty Questions, I Spy, or — her new favorite — Dog Breed Bingo, which she had made up. She and Charles were playing it right now.

After a while, Lizzie looked back at the card in her lap. PEKINGESE, BULLDOG, POODLE, HUSKY, SHAR-PEI, it said. Lizzie had crossed off all the letters she had seen as they drove: the E's, the S's, and the O's. She had spotted a K at a gas station, an H on a hotel sign, and an R at a railroad crossing, and crossed those off, too. She glanced at Charles's card. His read: DACHSHUND, ST. BERNARD, LABRADOR, DALMATIAN, BEAGLE. He had a lot of letters crossed off, but not as many as she did. She had a good feeling that she was going to be the first to cross off all the letters in one of her breeds. Yay!

As she watched, Charles crossed off all three of his *B*'s. Eek! Thanks to the Bean's help, he was getting closer. Lizzie crossed off her *B*, too, then stared out the window, concentrating hard. All she needed was a *U* and she'd win.

Then a big truck rumbled by. LABORATORY SUP-PLY said a big sign on its side.

"Husky!" yelled Lizzie, one second before Charles yelled, "Labrador!"

"I win!" Lizzie threw her fists in the air. "Whoo-hoo!"

"It was a tie." Charles stared at her in dis-belief.

"No way!" Lizzie wasn't about to give up her big victory. "I said my breed first."

Charles shook his head. "I said 'Lab' at the same time," he insisted.

Lizzie started to say something, but Mom

turned around in her seat. "No fighting, you guys, okay? You've been doing great so far. Call this one a tie and move on."

Lizzie grumbled, but she knew there was no point in arguing with Mom. Anyway, now they could both read the information on the back of their cards. That was the best part of the game. She turned her card over and started reading out loud. "'Husky,'" she read. "'A breed well suited for northern climates, with its thick undercoat for warmth and wide paws for good traction on snow.'" Lizzie practically knew all this by heart, even before she'd copied it off her "Dog Breeds of the World" poster. But she still loved reading it. "'Huskies, both the Siberian and Alaskan types, are known for their stamina and are widely used as sled dogs.'"

"What's 'stamina'?" asked Charles.

Lizzie rolled her eyes. "It's, you know . . ." She knew what it meant, but she couldn't exactly put it into words.

Dad came to her rescue. "It means energy that lasts and lasts."

"Like the Bean when he doesn't want to take his nap and he's acting like a *jumping* bean," Mom added with a smile.

"Yeah!" The Bean bumped up and down in his car seat. "I'm a *jumpin'* bean!"

Charles flipped his card over. "'Labrador retriever,'" he read. "'A strong, athletic dog with a friendly temperament. This breed is used as a hunting dog, a guide dog, and a family pet. Labs can be black, brown (also known as chocolate), or yellow.'"

"Like Honey!" said the Bean.

"Did you hear that?" Lizzie was impressed. "The Bean really knows his dog breeds." She beamed at her little brother. The Bean actually remembered that Honey, the last puppy the Petersons had fostered, was a yellow Lab!

The Petersons took care of puppies that needed homes, keeping each one until they could find it the perfect forever family. That's what fostering meant. Honey was one of their biggest success stories. She was going to learn how to be a service dog who could help a person in a wheelchair!

Buddy, the Petersons' own puppy, was another foster puppy success story. Once, Lizzie and her family had taken care of Buddy, his two sisters, and his mother. Four dogs! That was quite a responsibility. They had found other homes for Buddy's mom and his sisters, but they had all fallen in love with Buddy. Now Buddy was the Petersons' forever dog!

Lizzie felt sad thinking about Buddy. That was the only bad part about this vacation: Buddy could not come. He was staying with Lizzie's aunt Amanda, who ran a doggy day-care center and had four dogs of her own. Buddy loved Aunt Amanda, and staying with her and her dogs would be like a fun vacation for him. Lizzie knew he would be totally safe and very happy, but she still missed him. Right at that moment she would have loved to kiss his little nose and stroke his soft brown fur. She wished she could trace the white heart-shaped patch on his chest.

Lizzie looked out the window to distract herself. Eventually Dad turned off the interstate onto a smaller road, and suddenly everything started to look different. "Hey." Lizzie sat up straight. "Snow!" There was tons of the stuff! White, white, white, as far as her eyes could see. The sides of the road were piled high with snow. It covered the trees and the hills and even the tops of other cars that passed them.

"Yeah!" Dad said from up front. "Looks like they got walloped up here."

"Walloped!" yelled the Bean. Lizzie was sure her little brother had no idea Dad was saying that the area had been hit hard by a snowstorm. The Bean just loved to repeat what other people said.

"Walloped." Lizzie repeated it softly as she

looked out at all the snow. This vacation was going to be a real adventure. She could feel it in her bones.

Soon Lizzie spotted a sign, a big yellow arrow with red letters. It stood out against the white snow, pointing the way up a long dirt driveway lined with huge old trees. "Dad, look! Harris House Bed and Breakfast!" That was where they were staying.

Dad turned onto the road and pulled the van up to an old yellow farmhouse with a big red barn. The buildings looked cozy, with their roofs blanketed in thick snow. Someone must have seen them arrive, because a few seconds later the back door of the house flew open. "Wait! No! Bear, come!" a woman called.

Lizzie smiled as she watched a fluffy puppy bounce down the stairs and run straight for the van. "Look!" she said. "It's a husky!"

CHAPTER TWO

Lizzie unbuckled her seat belt, slid the door open, and started to hop out of the van.

"Careful!" Mom warned. "It might be sli —"

Too late. Lizzie slipped and slid on the snow-and-ice-packed driveway. She lost her balance but caught herself before she fell. "Whoa!" She grabbed the door handle.

"Watch it." The woman had picked her way close enough to grab the puppy and scoop him up. "Are you okay?"

Lizzie nodded, but she wasn't looking at the woman. She gazed at the adorable puppy in the woman's arms. He was so cute! His fur was fluffy, mostly black and gray with white markings. He had a pointy nose like the Big Bad

Wolf's, and triangular ears, one of which stood up while the other flopped over. His face was mostly white, with black around the eyes so that he looked as if he were wearing an old-fashioned burglar's mask. And the most amazing thing? One eye was brown, and the other was bright blue. Lizzie could not stop staring.

The woman laughed. "I know, isn't he cute? This is Bear." By then, Dad and Charles had climbed out of the van, and Mom was helping the Bean out of his car seat.

"You must be the Petersons. I'm Cordelia Harris." The woman smiled around at everyone. "I'm the sister who paints."

Lizzie remembered Mom mentioning that the bed-and-breakfast was run by two sisters, one who was a painter and one who was a musician. She liked Cordelia Harris right away. Cordelia had red cheeks and long, thick brown braids, and she wore a big, fuzzy, multicolored sweater.

"Dorothy is inside, practicing. And she just finished baking some cookies," Cordelia went on.

"Cookies!" The Bean's face lit up. "Gimme cookies!"

"What do you say?" Mom reminded him.

"*Lots* of cookies!" yelled the Bean. Then, when Mom gave him a look, he added, "Please?" He gave Cordelia his best "aren't-I-the-cutest?" smile.

"You can have as many cookies as your mom and dad allow," said Cordelia. "Now, come on in, everybody, before you all freeze!" She led the way up the snowy front walk, still carrying the puppy.

Inside, it was deliciously warm. Lizzie stopped to pull off her jacket. She heard the sound of a tinkling piano — and then silence. In a moment, a woman appeared. She looked just like Cordelia, except that her braids were more gray than brown. "Welcome," she said. "I'm Dorothy. Please, come on into the parlor." She led them into a room full of overstuffed armchairs, with paintings on the walls and richly colored rugs on the floor. A big fire crackled away in a giant stone fireplace. A piano stood in one corner, and there were shelves and shelves full of books. Lizzie spotted a plate of chocolate-chip cookies on a big round wooden table, with a teapot and mugs beside it.

"Now this looks relaxing." Mom beamed as Cordelia waved them in and invited them to sit down.

Just then, the little husky pup wriggled out of Cordelia's arms, jumped down onto the floor, wandered over to the fireplace, and curled up for a nap.

"Awww!" Lizzie could not believe how cute he was. "He's sleepy!"

"Lazy is more like it." Dorothy snorted. "That's why he's here."

"What do you mean?" Dad asked.

"We're just taking care of Bear," said Cordelia. "He doesn't belong to us. In fact, he's looking for a home."

Lizzie and Charles stared at each other. They had come all the way to Vermont, only to meet a puppy like all the others they had fostered back home — a puppy who needed a forever family. "What does laziness have to do with it?" Lizzie went over to sit in front of the fire near Bear and stroke his long, soft fur.

"A musher friend of ours dropped Bear off a couple of weeks ago," Dorothy said.

"Musher?" Charles asked. "Like — oatmeal?"

Cordelia laughed. "Up here, musher means sled-dog racer. You know, like 'Mush! Mush!' Only, they don't really say that to get their dogs moving. That's kind of a myth."

Dorothy passed the plate of cookies. "So Bruce, our friend, raises sled dogs and races them. Bear was part of the last litter of puppies, and Bruce felt that he just really didn't fit in. He said Bear was too unmotivated and would never make a good sled dog."

Lizzie drew in a breath. "That's mean."

"Actually, it's just the truth." Cordelia shrugged. "You can see for yourself. He likes to greet our guests, but besides that, all he wants to do is eat and sleep."

"There's another reason our friend had to leave him with us," said Dorothy. "He couldn't take care of a puppy right now. Bruce had to leave town —"

"That's no excuse for abandoning a puppy —" Lizzie began.

But Dorothy finished, "— because he's headed for Alaska, to run the Iditarod."

Lizzie's jaw fell open. "Really? That's — that's so cool! My class just did a whole unit on the Iditarod."

"Ibibabob!" echoed the Bean, dancing around excitedly. "Dabibalod! Gaboogidog!"

"The *what*?" Charles asked.

"Eye-*dit*-uh-rod," Lizzie pronounced the word carefully. "It's a race. The longest, wildest sled-dog race in the world."

"That's right." Dorothy nodded. "It goes from Anchorage to Nome, through some of the deepest wilderness in the world."

"The race is over a thousand miles long!" said Lizzie. "And it's very historical. A long time ago there was this disease called — um —"

"Diphtheria," Dorothy put in. "It was a bad disease, especially for young people. And there was no way to get the medicine to those who needed it way up in Nome. So they sent it by dogsled."

"Yeah." Lizzie remembered the whole story. "And it was, like, forty below zero, and it took six days! And one of the dogs was named Balto. There's a statue of him in New York City."

"That's right," said Dorothy. "And nowadays they run the Iditarod as a race every year, to honor Balto and the other brave dogs."

"Cool," said Charles.

"Very good, Lizzie," said Mom. "Sounds like you really learned about this topic."

Lizzie always had an excellent memory for anything that had to do with dogs. She patted Bear again, and he yawned and licked her hand. His fluffy fur was warm from the fire. No way was this sleepy puppy ready to help pull a dogsled for over one thousand miles. "I guess Bear does need another home," she said. "Maybe we can help find him one!"

CHAPTER THREE

"I still can't believe you managed to find a puppy to foster all the way up here in Vermont." Mom shook her head at Lizzie the next morning.

Lizzie sat by the fireplace with a belly full of the best waffles she'd ever had. She brushed Bear gently, combing tiny snarls out of his coat. "I know!" Lizzie grinned. "Isn't it great?"

Mom sighed. "Well, it's not necessarily what I would choose for *my* vacation, but I know it makes you happy to have a puppy to care for. And I must admit he's very cute. Being around him helps me miss Buddy a little less."

She came over to pat Bear. "Hi, Beary." Mom spoke softly. "You're a little sweetie, aren't you?"

Bear yawned.

Whatever you say. Can I go back to my nap now?

"Cordelia says that even if he is lazy, he's smart," Lizzie reported. "She said he's completely house-trained — he goes right out into the snow to do his business. She said he doesn't mind the snow and cold at all — that he would probably *live* outside, if he could."

Mom raised her eyebrows. "Bear may like the cold, but he sure seems to like snoozing by the fireplace, too!" She laughed. "I can relate. I could almost curl up for a nap on that couch over there. It's so cozy in here."

Just then Dad came downstairs, all dressed for cross-country skiing in wool pants and a puffy red vest over a gray wool sweater. Behind him were Charles and the Bean, who were also bundled up and ready to go. "Let's hit the trails!" Dad looked eager. "I've got our skis all ready."

Lizzie groaned. She really just wanted to lie by the fire, tickling Bear's pink puppy belly.

"Come on." Dad ignored the groan. "It'll be fun. It's supposed to start snowing really hard later today, so now's the perfect time to learn the basics. Then tomorrow we'll have a whole pile of beautiful new snow to play in."

"Come on." Mom poked Lizzie with her foot. "We'll have a good time. And Bear will be right here waiting for you when we get back."

Lizzie gave Bear one more kiss. "Okay." She was already mostly dressed — all she had to do was pull on her snow pants and jacket and she'd be ready. When Dad saw how terrible she was at skiing, maybe she could spend the rest of the vacation playing with Bear.

"Have fun." Cordelia waved from her painting studio on the sunporch as the Petersons headed out the back door.

"Don't forget your trail map." Dorothy ran after

them with a pamphlet in her hand. "Our trail goes right through the woods until it meets a snowmobile trail that you can follow for miles."

"Thanks." Dad put the map in his pocket. "Cordelia showed me the best route this morning. We should be back by lunchtime. If we're not, send out the Mounties."

"Keep an eye on the sky." Dorothy squinted up at the low gray clouds overhead. "I have a feeling that storm may begin a little earlier than the weatherman said."

Great. Now Lizzie had to worry about getting lost in a blizzard, on top of everything else.

Mom began to settle the Bean into the little sled he'd be riding in, towed behind her or Dad. And Dad helped Charles and Lizzie put on their skis. "Just step down right here." He guided the toe of Lizzie's ski boot into the ski's binding. "Hear that click? That means you're all locked in and ready to roll."

Charles had both skis on in no time. He started sliding around the yard like a maniac. "Look at me! Look at me! I'm doing it!"

Show-off, Lizzie thought. Then, without any warning, she fell down. She hadn't even been doing anything. Just standing there! Now, she was on her side in the snow, with her legs and feet and skis all tangled up. She couldn't even begin to figure out how to untangle them. Not only that, but Dad was laughing at her.

She glared at him, and he stopped. He helped her untangle her legs and held out a hand so he could help haul her to her feet. "Sorry." He was still smiling. "It's just that I've done that exact thing myself so many times. It's embarrassing. But kind of funny, really. One minute you're standing there, the next you're not." He helped her get her hat back on straight and gave her a kiss on the cheek. "Try again. It's really not so hard. All you do is push off with one foot and glide on the other ski. See?" He started to ski around her in a big circle. "Kick, glide. Kick, glide." He made it look easy.

Lizzie grabbed her ski poles, which seemed way too long and in the way, and tried to shove off. Kick, glide. How hard could it be? Charles and Mom, towing the Bean, were already on their way down the trail that led through the woods in back of the farmhouse. Dad waited patiently. "That's it," he called. "You've got it!"

For a second, Lizzie felt her skis glide silently over the silky snow. For a second, she felt the crisp, cold winter air against her cheeks. For a second, she flew!

Oof. Down she went again.

Dad came over to help her up.

They continued that way for what seemed like hours. Lizzie fell every few minutes and Dad helped her up but they kept moving along. Soon it started to snow. Suddenly, big snowflakes swirled all around, so thickly that Lizzie couldn't even see Charles and Mom up ahead anymore. She could barely make out the trees on either side of the trail. She felt like she was inside her own giant-sized snow globe.

"You know what?" Lizzie began, after she fell for the fortieth time. She was about to tell Dad that maybe he should go on without her. She had tried, but it was obvious that cross-country ski-ing was not her thing. Really, she would rather sit by the fire with Bear in her lap. And wouldn't Dad rather be off kicking and gliding with the others, instead of constantly untangling her and picking her up off the snow?

But before Lizzie could say a thing, Dorothy zoomed up to them, racing fast on her own long wooden skis, her braids flying behind her.

"Have you seen Bear?" Her face was bright red and her eyes were bright. "He's lost!"

CHAPTER FOUR

"Lost? Oh, no! What do you mean, Bear is lost?" Lizzie didn't understand.

"I was welcoming some new guests, and Bear ran out of the house" — Dorothy gasped, a little out of breath — "just like he did yesterday. This time I had clipped on his little red leash, but he pulled it out of my hands. By the time I got the guests settled inside, Bear was — he was nowhere to be found. I thought he might have followed you, but there's no sign of him along the trail."

"We'll find him," Dad said. "Don't worry. How far could he have gone?" He turned to Lizzie. "You head on back with Dorothy. I'll go tell Mom and Charles what's up." He skied off fast, disappearing into the flying snow.

Lizzie didn't know how she managed, but she skied back to Harris House without falling. Maybe she was getting the hang of it. Or maybe she was just so worried about Bear that her fear kept her going. "Could Bear have wandered into the road?" she asked.

"I don't even want to think about that." Dorothy closed her eyes tightly. "Maybe he'll be safe and sound inside when we get back."

But he wasn't.

Cordelia met them at the back door. "Any sign of Bear?" She wrung her hands.

Dorothy shook her head. "It's snowing too hard. Any trail he would have left is already covered." She reached down to undo her ski bindings. "Can you grab a few pairs of snowshoes?" Cordelia disappeared inside.

Dorothy helped Lizzie out of her skis. "Snowshoes will be easier to get around on."

Cordelia reappeared with an armful of big wooden snowshoes. "I'll set the extras out here."

She piled several pairs by the back door. "I called Tim Carter. He's busy, but he said he'd send his daughter over to help."

"Neighbors." Dorothy showed Lizzie how to strap on a pair of snowshoes. "They live down the road. We all help one another out up here."

By the time Lizzie and Cordelia had gotten their snowshoes on, Dad was back. "Mom and Charles are on their way." He was panting a little. "Where should I start looking?"

"Maybe you could ski the other way down the trail, toward town." Cordelia pointed. "The rest of us will search the woods around the house. Oh, good, here's Fern."

A teenage girl dashed around the corner of the farmhouse, wearing snowshoes — sleek, modern metal ones with red bindings — and a bright red jacket. "Dad said your dog is lost."

"Not our dog —" Dorothy began to explain that they were just taking care of Bear temporarily, but then she shook her head. "Yes. A little husky pup. Named Bear. Lizzie, this is Fern Carter. Fern, Lizzie Peterson. Why don't you two search around the back of the barn and in the apple orchard?"

"Umm . . ." Lizzie was about to say she didn't know where the apple orchard was, but Fern was already on her way toward the big red barn.

"She knows her way around." Dorothy gave Lizzie a little push. "Stick with Fern and you won't get lost in the snow."

Lizzie remembered a scene in *The Long Winter*, one of her favorite Laura Ingalls Wilder books, where there was a big blizzard, with snow so thick and heavy that Laura had to hang on to a rope to find her way between the house and the barn. Fern's red jacket had almost disappeared into the swirling flakes. "Wait up!" Lizzie yelled. She took three steps on her snowshoes and fell face-first into the snow. "Argh!"

"Take it easy at first." Dorothy helped Lizzie

up. "You'll get used to those snowshoes quickly. But it's a little different from walking normally. You have to walk kind of like a duck, with your feet apart." She demonstrated with a few waddling steps. "Now, let's find that pup."

"Bear!" Lizzie waddled after Fern, trying to keep the red jacket in sight. "Beary boy! Where are you? Come, Bear!"

Lizzie caught up to Fern and they snowshoed all the way around the barn. Then they went along an old stone wall that ran by a group of small trees with twisty, tangled branches, just like the scary apple trees that come to life in *The Wizard of Oz*. They yelled and yelled, calling Bear's name over and over.

Lizzie only fell once, but that was embarrassing enough. "Graceful." Fern said it with a smile, but Lizzie felt like an idiot. Fern ran around on her snowshoes as if she'd been doing it all her life, which she probably had. It wasn't very nice of her to make fun of people who were new at it. But there was no time to stew about hurt feelings. They had to find Bear.

"Let's look inside the barn." Fern pushed the big door open. "He might have wriggled inside somehow, looking for shelter." Lizzie peeked over Fern's shoulder. It was very dark and very quiet in there, and it smelled just like the horse barn where Lizzie sometimes rode with her friend Maria. Like old, dusty hay and animals. The smell reminded Lizzie of Rascal, the wild little puppy who had found a wonderful home at that stable. She smiled for just a second — then she remembered about Bear.

"I don't think he's in here." Lizzie shook her head. "He'd come running if he heard us. Or we'd hear him crying if he was stuck somewhere."

"Anyway, it's too dark to search without a flashlight. We can come back later if we need to. But let's go back to the house and see if there's any news yet," Fern suggested. They headed toward the parking area near the front door.

Lizzie looked at the house. She remembered how Bear had run out to greet them the day before. Where, oh, where, was that cute little puppy now? She felt her throat close up and she blinked back some tears. Then she remembered something else. The house had looked different yesterday. Or at least the *roof* had.

"Fern." She tugged on the sleeve of the older girl's jacket. "Look!" Lizzie pointed toward the green metal roof over the front door.

"What?" Fern asked. "Do you see Bear?"

Lizzie shook her head. "No. But yesterday, when we got here, that green roof wasn't showing. It was covered with snow. And now look!" She pointed to a huge mountain of snow that must have just slid off the roof. It came all the way up to the parlor windows. "What if Bear was right by the door when —"

But Fern wasn't even listening anymore. She charged toward the house.

CHAPTER FIVE

Lizzie ran after Fern, stumbling on her snow-shoes. When they got to the house, each girl grabbed one of the big metal snow shovels propped by the door. They began to flail away, trying to chop through the towering piles of snow that had slid off the roof. Lizzie was surprised by how dense — icy and heavy — the old snow was. It wasn't at all like the fluffy fresh snow that fell all around them.

The door flew open. "What's going on?" Cordelia stared at the girls.

"Bear might be under here!" Lizzie didn't even stop digging. "This snow just slid off the roof today."

Cordelia's hand flew to her mouth. "Oh, my." She closed the door for a moment, then reappeared wearing a jacket. She pulled on a pair of leather work gloves. "I'll take a turn with one of those shovels." She held out her hand.

Lizzie handed over her shovel. Her arms were already sore. She walked away from the spot where they'd been digging and tilted her head toward the pile of snow. "Bear?" She tried to listen. "Are you in there?" Lizzie's heart thumped. How could such a little puppy survive if all that heavy snow fell on him?

Then she thought she heard something. A whimper? Could it be? She held up her hand. "Stop for a sec!" When the shoveling noises stopped, the other noise became clearer. "Bear?" Lizzie could hardly speak. "Is that you?"

She heard another, louder whimper.

Lizzie bent to look beneath a huge slab of hardened snow. She saw one little blue eye peering back at her. Could it be? Yes, it was him! The puppy was trapped in a little cave that must have been created when the snow slid off the roof. "Bear!" Lizzie threw herself down and peered into the space. "It's him." Lizzie turned to face the others. "Bear! Over here! I can see him. He's under this slab."

Cordelia and Fern ran over with their shovels and began to chip away at the chunks of snow. "Faster!" Lizzie urged. "He might be hurt." She bent closer to whisper to Bear. "We'll save you, don't worry."

Dad skied into the yard. He undid his bindings and ran over. "Bear's under there?"

Cordelia nodded. "Lizzie can see him. But the snow is so hard right here. If we could only move this whole big slab —"

Dad grabbed the two snow shovels and shoved the end of each one under the slab. "Lizzie, get ready to push down on that one." He bent all his weight over his shovel's handle, and Lizzie hunched over hers. "One, two, three — push!"

The slab didn't budge at first. Then it seemed to unlock from its frozen position. As it rocked up at an angle, Lizzie caught a glimpse of something black and gray and white and fluffy. "Bear!" She felt tears spring to her eyes. "Oh, Bear."

Cordelia reached in and snatched Bear out of his safe little cave. Lizzie and Dad let the slab fall back into place.

"Is he okay?" Lizzie reached out to him gently. "Is he hurt?"

Cordelia ran her hands all over Bear's furry body. "I don't think so." She looked up at Lizzie. "Can you believe it? I think he's totally fine!"

"He doesn't even look very scared." Fern patted him, too. "Look, he's yawning. What an adorable puppy!"

Dorothy brought out a blanket and wrapped Bear up tight. Sure enough, his pink tongue lolled out as he lay back in Cordelia's arms, looking completely relaxed and happy.

What's all the fuss? I knew you'd find me. So, is it time for dinner, or what?

Lizzie had to smile. Bear was a cool character, all right. Nothing seemed to rattle him. She kissed his soft furry face, and he licked her cheek.

"And it was Lizzie who figured out where he was!" Later, Dad called Aunt Amanda. He told her all about the day's adventures. "Lizzie was the hero."

Lizzie sat by the fire with Bear on her lap. She blushed. She didn't *feel* like a hero. But she sure was glad that Bear was safe. Even Fern had said Lizzie was "brilliant" to have noticed how the snow had slid off the roof.

"Ask how Buddy is." Lizzie waved at her dad. "Is he by the phone? Can I talk to him?" Something about Bear's scary adventure made Lizzie miss her puppy terribly. That's why she had asked Dad to call Aunt Amanda.

Dad gestured to Lizzie. "He's waiting to hear your voice." He brought her the phone.

"Buddy? Is that you? Who's a good little boy?" Lizzie heard a little snuffling sound on the other end. "Buddy?"

Aunt Amanda spoke up. "You should see him. His head is tilted in that really cute way. He definitely recognizes your voice." She laughed. "So, how's the skiing?"

Lizzie groaned. "I'm terrible at it," she said. "All I do is fall down. But Charles is really good already!"

"Oh, well. Everybody's got *something* they're good at. It's just a matter of finding the best fit for you." Then Aunt Amanda giggled. "Buddy's licking my chin."

Lizzie laughed. "Give him a kiss for me, okay?"

"I will," Aunt Amanda promised. "And you tell that cute little Bear to stay out of trouble."

CHAPTER SIX

Lizzie gasped when she looked out her window the next morning. Snow covered everything in sight: the barn roof, the fences, the cars, the driveway, the mailbox. The snow was like a thick, fluffy quilt, outlining every tiny twig of every branch of every tree. Not only that, the sky was blue and the sun was shining, making the snow glitter like diamonds. It was like a fairyland.

Downstairs, Dad raced through his breakfast. "I can't wait to get out there. The skiing should be fantastic today."

"Yeah! Skiing." The Bean waved a half-eaten pancake in the air.

"You want to ride in your sled again, don't you?" Mom wiped syrup off his fingers.

The Bean nodded and smiled. "Yup. Skiing."

"I'll go," Charles said. "I want to ski all the way around that long trail today."

Lizzie looked down at her plate and drew her fork through a puddle of leftover syrup. Cordelia passed her a platter full of pancakes, offering seconds, but Lizzie had lost her appetite. "No, thanks." She put down her fork. Everybody in her family was good at skiing — except her. Lizzie felt left out.

"You know," Dorothy leaned toward Lizzie, "I'd be glad to loan you those snowshoes again if you'd like to take Bear out for a walk."

"Really?"

"You'd be doing us a favor." Cordelia agreed with her sister. "We've got a lot of cooking and cleaning to do today, and he's just going to be underfoot."

Lizzie beamed. "I'd be happy to!"

"Just make sure you hold on to his leash."

Dorothy smiled at Lizzie. "We don't want a repeat of yesterday."

"I promise." Lizzie crossed her heart.

As soon as she finished breakfast, Lizzie went to find Bear. He was snoozing by the fireplace again, but when she asked if he'd like to go for a walk, he got to his feet and stretched, yawned a big pink yawn, and waved his fluffy tail in the air.

I'll go anywhere with you!

Lizzie pulled on her snow pants, jacket, and boots. She clipped on Bear's red leash, then picked him up and tucked him inside her jacket with his head poking out. "I'll carry you for a little while."

Bear snuggled down cozily.

This is nice! More nap time for me.

By the time Lizzie got her snowshoes fastened, the rest of her family had taken off down the trail on their skis. "Be careful," Mom called as she skied out of view, towing the Bean behind her. *Careful of* what? Lizzie thought. The storm was over, the sun was bright, and the only sound was the cheeping of the adorable little chickadees that flittered around the Harris sisters' bird feeder.

Lizzie tromped across the yard on her snowshoes, feeling the warm weight of Bear nestled inside her jacket. It was fun to be off on an adventure of her own. She decided to try a different trail from the day before, just to see where it led. Cordelia had promised that she couldn't get lost, since all the trails eventually circled back to the house.

The snow was light and fluffy, and when a little breeze shook it off the trees, it looked like diamond dust sparkling all around. Lizzie took a deep breath of the fresh, cold air. She *liked* it up here in Vermont.

When she got to the main trail, Lizzie turned right instead of following her family's ski tracks to the left, the way she and Dad had gone the day before. "Let's explore, Bear." She unzipped her jacket and carefully lowered Bear to the snow. She held tightly on to his leash.

Lizzie trudged along quietly for a while and Bear romped beside her. He seemed totally at home in the snow. Once in a while he would duck his head and lick up a few flakes, or stick his nose into a soft snowbank and sniff hard, then jump back with a big sneeze, or fall onto his back and roll around happily, his pink tongue lolling out as he grinned up at Lizzie.

Welcome to my winter world!

Bear seemed to come to life when he was outside. No more yawning and napping. Now he zigged and zagged across the trail in front of Lizzie, pulling her along as he sniffed at this and that. Then he began to pull harder, his nose to the ground and his tail held high. He sniffed harder than ever.

"What are you smelling?" Hadn't Cordelia mentioned something about a moose that hung around sometimes? Lizzie wasn't sure exactly what a moose looked like, but she knew they were huge. Bigger than horses. What if she ran into one, out here all alone? She remembered reading that the sled-dog racers in the Iditarod were always worried about meeting a moose on the trail.

Bear stood still for a moment and sniffed the air. His ears were on full alert. Lizzie could tell that he was using his super doggy senses to hear something that she could not hear and smell something she could not smell. Then Bear pulled so hard that he pulled Lizzie right off balance. She plopped down into the deep, unpacked snow on the side of the trail, still gripping the leash.

Lizzie struggled to get her snowshoes underneath her so she could stand up again. Bear pulled at the leash some more. His ears twitched madly as he sniffed and snuffled. Finally, Lizzie got to her feet. She could hear something, too. What was that? It sounded like a huge animal running down the trail toward her and Bear, breathing hard but moving silently.

Was it a moose? Lizzie almost didn't want to look up as the breathing came closer.

CHAPTER SEVEN

Lizzie scooped Bear into her arms. She stepped off the trail and tried to hide behind a tree. She squinched her eyes shut. But then her curiosity got the better of her.

She opened her eyes.

And Lizzie saw the most amazing thing: a team of sled dogs, pulling a wooden sled!

A person in a red jacket stood on the sled's runners. The dogs looked just like grown-up Bears. They weren't barking or whining. They just trotted happily along, breathing hard in the cold, crisp air. Now that they were closer, Lizzie could hear the jingling of the tags on their collars.

"Easy! Easy, Denali! Easy, Sitka! Easy, dogs!"

Lizzie thought that voice was familiar. The dogs slowed to a stop, then stood panting. The driver tossed a big metal hook onto the snow. It was attached to a rope, like a ship's anchor.

Bear was *entranced*. Lizzie let him down. He stared at the dogs, his tail wagging madly as he strained at the leash.

Wow! You guys are the coolest. I wish I could do that.

This was the most excited Lizzie had ever seen Bear. She tightened her grip on his leash. It was embarrassing enough to be hiding behind a tree without having her dog run off.

"Need some help?"

Now Lizzie remembered where she had heard that voice before. The sled driver was Fern! Of all people. Now Lizzie was really embarrassed. Fern was going to make fun of her again. "I'm — I'm fine," she said, even though she was floundering in the deep snow on the side of the trail.

"Those big, old-fashioned snowshoes are *impossible*. I trip and fall all the time when I wear them." Fern grinned and stuck out a hand. "Come on."

Maybe Fern wasn't going to laugh at her. Maybe Fern was okay after all. Lizzie took the older girl's hand and Fern pulled her back onto the trail.

"You're a sled-dog driver?" Lizzie couldn't believe it. How cool.

"Yep, I'm a musher." Fern bent to say hello to Bear. "Hey, little sweetie! You seem to be totally recovered from your big adventure." She petted him, then straightened up and looked at Lizzie. "I've helped raise a lot of dogs, but this little guy is really something special. He's so confident."

"I know." Lizzie was about to ask if Fern knew anyone who was looking for a puppy, but Fern spoke up first.

"How about a ride?"

"Me? On the dogsled?" Lizzie stared at Fern. "Really?"

"Sure, why not? My dogs and I have been out for a couple of hours, so they're tired and not nearly as wild as they can sometimes be. If we'd met you earlier in our run, I never would have been able to stop them, not even with my snow hook." Fern yanked on the rope.

So *that's* what the big metal anchor-thing was called. Lizzie looked at the wooden sled and then back at Fern. "So, I would ride in the sled while you stand behind me?"

"That's right." Fern smiled at Bear. "And you can tuck little Bear into your jacket so he'll be safe. I have a feeling he'll enjoy the ride, too."

Fern walked Lizzie up the line of dogs. "These are Denali and Sitka, my lead dogs." She pointed to each one. "Behind them are Kodiak and Juneau. And then we have Koyuk and Homer."

Lizzie thought the dogs were beautiful, every

one of them. Some had one blue eye, just like Bear. They had curly tails like his, and pointy noses, and pointy ears. They were long-legged, strong-looking dogs. "Are these all huskies?" Lizzie thought they looked a little different from the husky on her Dog Breeds poster.

Fern nodded. "They're Alaskan huskies, like Bear. Some people use Siberian huskies for their sled teams, but my dad and I like Alaskans. Some people say Alaskans are faster, some people say Siberians can run forever. I like Alaskans because they're basically mutts. Their ancestors are Alaskan village dogs, with all sorts of other breeds thrown into the mix. Hunting hounds, Siberians, malamutes, even greyhounds!"

Lizzie was fascinated. She was about to ask some more questions, but Fern guided her toward the sled. Some of the dogs were starting to bark and jump around. "The dogs are getting restless." Fern grabbed the sled. "We'd better get going, or they'll take off without us!"

Lizzie unbuckled her snowshoes and Fern stowed them behind the passenger part of the sled. Then Lizzie tucked Bear into her jacket and zipped it up tight so he couldn't wriggle out. She climbed into the sled. Her heart beat quickly. She couldn't believe she was about to take a dog-sled ride.

Fern tucked a blanket around Lizzie. "All set?" Lizzie nodded. "I think so."

"Keep your hands inside the sled," Fern advised. She climbed onto the runners behind Lizzie and pulled up the snow hook. "Hike!" she cried. "Let's go!"

Immediately, the dogs strained at their harnesses. Lizzie felt a thrill run through her whole body as the sled began to move. In a moment, the dogs were trotting quickly. They charged up the path with the sled gliding behind them.

Lizzie's eyes filled with tears. She wasn't sure why exactly. It wasn't the cold breeze in her face. It was that it was just so — so beautiful, so wonderful, to be flying through the snowy woods, watching the dogs run. Their tongues flapped in the cold air as they worked together as a perfect team. "Wow." Lizzie felt completely happy. "Wow!"

"I know." Fern spoke up behind her. "Isn't it amazing? I've wanted to do this ever since I was a little girl and Dad told me about Susan Butcher. She won the Iditarod four times! Now I'm in training myself, for the Junior Iditarod. Next year Dad and I are both going to Alaska. He's been training for years, and he thinks he and his team are ready."

"Wow." Lizzie hugged Bear's warm, heavy puppy body to her chest. She could hear his little heart beating extra fast. Instead of curling up for a nap, he kept his head poked out of the top of Lizzie's jacket. He watched every move the sled dogs made. Lizzie leaned back on the sled as the dogs galloped down a hill, sending chunks of snow flying.

The ride was over way too soon. Fern drove the dogs right up to Harris House. Mom, Dad, Charles, and the Bean, who had just returned from their ski tour, stood and stared as Lizzie climbed out of the sled.

"That was awesome!" Lizzie grinned at Fern. "Thank you so, so much."

"Why don't you and Bear come over to our place tomorrow?" Fern had one foot off the sled, holding the dogs back. "You can meet my dad and all our other dogs. We can even go for another ride." She grinned and waved at Lizzie's family. Then she hopped back onto the sled, and with a "Hike!" and a wave, she was gone.

CHAPTER EIGHT

Cordelia drove Lizzie and Bear over to Fern's house right after breakfast the next morning. This time, Lizzie didn't mind at all that the rest of her family would be skiing. In fact, this time Lizzie could tell that Charles was a little jealous of her as she climbed into Cordelia's old beat-up pickup truck. "You'll get a ride tomorrow," she reminded him as she waved good-bye. When Fern's dad had called to make arrangements for Lizzie's visit, he had offered to take all the Petersons out for a dogsled ride. Charles and the Bean were pretty excited about that.

"I had a feeling that you and Fern would hit it off." Cordelia turned up a long, rutted dirt driveway a few minutes later. "She's dog-crazy, just like you! Maybe you can convince her and her dad to adopt Bear. Wouldn't that be great?" She pulled up to a small log cabin next to a big barn. Lizzie could hear dogs barking.

"That's exactly what I've been thinking." Lizzie smiled at Cordelia. "I'll do my best." She climbed out of the truck, holding Bear's leash.

"Call me if you need a ride back!" Cordelia drove off with a wave.

Fern came outside. "Welcome to Dog Central." She waved a hand at the huge fenced-in area between the cabin and the barn.

Lizzie felt like she was in dog heaven. There seemed to be *dozens* of dogs out there! Dogs were running, playing, rolling on their backs in the snow. "We don't like to keep our dogs tied up." Fern led Lizzie toward the barn. "They can roam around anywhere inside the fence. And they're welcome in the house. Last night I ended up sleeping on the floor because Homer and Sitka claimed my bed." Fern knelt down to say hello to

Bear. "Hi, sweetie!" She picked him up so she could nuzzle his neck.

"You know" — Lizzie decided to grab the moment — "Bear needs a home."

"He *does*?" Fern's eyes lit up. "Maybe my dad will —"

"'Maybe my dad will *what*?" said a deep voice behind Lizzie.

She turned to see a smiling man in brown coveralls.

"Lizzie, this is my dad." Fern introduced them. "Dad, this is Lizzie."

"Hi, Mr. Carter." Lizzie smiled.

"Call me Tim." The man stuck out a hand for a shake. "And who do we have here?" He reached over to scratch Bear between the ears.

"Dad, this is Bear." Fern spoke up. "And guess what? He's looking for a home."

Tim Carter frowned. "He looks like one of Bruce Madden's dogs."

Lizzie thought that name sounded familiar. "I

think he is. Bruce gave Bear to the Harrises to foster because he said Bear was unmoti —" She stopped. Suddenly, she thought better of telling Tim and Fern that Bruce thought Bear was lazy. "I mean, because Bruce had to go to Alaska for the Iditarod."

"Dad?" Fern looked up at her father. "Maybe Bear would fit in here with us."

Tim Carter eyed Bear suspiciously. "I don't think so." He shook his head. "Bruce already offered this pup to me, but I said no thanks. Why would I want to take on one of his rejects?"

"Please, Daddy?" Fern begged.

"We're already feeding twenty-eight dogs." Tim shook his head again. "You know I'm putting every spare cent toward our Iditarod goal. I can't afford to keep a dog that doesn't pull. And I'm too busy getting my own team trained. I can't take on a puppy now."

"But —" Fern began.

Tim held up his hand. "Enough, Fern. Speaking

of feeding, the dogs are hungry. I think you've got some chores to do." He nodded curtly to Lizzie, turned, and walked toward the cabin.

Fern gave Bear one last squeeze. "Sorry, sweetie." She kissed his face. "Sorry, Lizzie. I guess Dad's right. Bruce is the best musher around." Fern shrugged. "He's a real serious trainer, and he knows his dogs."

Fern put Bear back on the ground and handed his leash to Lizzie. "Want to meet the rest of our dogs? You can help me feed them."

She led Lizzie into the barn and introduced her to dog after dog. "This is Muffin," she said. "And Spud, and his brother Tater, and that's Lollipup, and T-Bone. Dad's always hungry, so all his dogs have food names — in case you didn't notice." While Lizzie petted the dogs and let them sniff Bear, Fern pulled out a couple of big buckets and started mixing. "We use high-protein kibble," she said. "Plus hunks of frozen salmon that we get from a guy in Canada. We mix it all up with warm water and this stinky fish oil that's supposed to be good for them." She poured a long glug from a big bottle into each bucket.

By now, there were a dozen dogs milling around, all hungry eyes and lolling tongues.

"Don't they ever get in fights?" Lizzie was trying to pat three dogs at once. How did Fern and her dad manage all these dogs?

Fern shook her head. "They all know who's boss." She pointed at a lanky black dog. "Muffin there, she runs the show. Nobody would ever mess with her. T-Bone is second in command. Every dog knows his or her place. That's why they don't care about Bear being here. They know he's just a pup and no threat."

Once they'd fed the dogs, Fern showed Lizzie where they kept their sleds — some for racing, some for training, some, like the one Lizzie had been on the day before, for giving rides. There was even a tandem sled, with room for two drivers. Fern said she had learned to mush on that sled, standing in front of her dad as they drove the dogs together.

Then they went into the harness room, where everything was neat and organized. The harnesses were hung in order of size, each with a plaque near it, listing the names of the dogs they fit. "'Muffin, Sitka, Waffle, Koyuk.'" Lizzie read the names on a plaque. She reached out to touch one of the harnesses, and three dogs ran over, tails wagging eagerly.

"They're dying to go out for a run," Fern said. "These dogs just *live* to pull. It's in their genes. Plus, we make it fun. Our training sessions are like playtime."

Lizzie looked down at Bear. He was on his hind legs, with his nose stretched way up high to sniff at a smaller set of harnesses whose plaques read: PEANUT, HOMER, SPUD. Bear's tail wagged just as hard as the big dogs'. "You know what?" Lizzie said. "I think that Bruce guy might be wrong about Bear. I think he might like to pull, too."

CHAPTER NINE

"What do you mean?" Fern sat down on a hay bale and pulled Bear onto her lap.

"Okay." Lizzie sat down next to her. "The truth is that Bruce told the Harris sisters that Bear was lazy and unmotivated. That's why he gave him up."

Fern nodded. "Bruce can't afford to keep a dog that doesn't pull, any more than we can."

"But you said that Bruce was a real serious trainer."

Fern nodded again. "He is. He keeps his dogs tied up whenever they're not working and never lets them in the house. And he's very strict. It works for him, though. He wins a lot of races around here."

"Well, I don't have any experience with sled dogs," Lizzie said, "but I have trained a lot of puppies. And one thing I've learned is that all puppies learn differently. Some learn quickly, some slowly. Some need lots of rules, and others need to be babied a little."

Fern's eyes lit up. "You mean — you think it's just that Bruce might not have been the right trainer for Bear?"

"Exactly." Lizzie was starting to talk faster now. "It's true that Bear likes to sleep in front of the fire, and he's not the most hyper dog I've ever seen. But you know when he's been the most excited? Every time he's around your dogs, that's when. He can't keep his eyes off them. And you should have seen him when he heard them coming down the trail yesterday. He pulled me right off my feet."

By the time Lizzie finished, Fern had jumped up. She shooed all the grown-up dogs outside and into their pen. Then she rummaged around in a big wooden box beneath the harness hooks. "I think this might fit him." She held up a tangle of purple nylon webbing. "This was Homer's puppy harness. We start play training our dogs really young."

"You mean —" Lizzie jumped up. "Can we try that on Bear? And see if he likes to pull?"

"I think we should try our training method and see if it works better than Bruce's." Fern nodded. "I think you might be right." She picked up Bear and spoke softly to him, petting him gently as she arranged the harness over his head. "See, the X goes over his back, and this part goes in front of his chest." She showed Lizzie. "Nothing goes around his neck, since a sled dog would never pull from there."

Bear's tail wagged hard.

Oh, boy. Oh, boy! Does this mean I get to run like the other dogs?

"So far, so good." Fern gave Bear a kiss on the nose. "He doesn't seem to mind the harness at all."

"What's next?" Lizzie was dying to know.

Fern rummaged in the big box again. She pulled out a long nylon rope and clipped it onto a ring on Bear's back. "Next we see how he likes the feeling of dragging the rope around." She put Bear down on the floor, then walked quickly to the other corner of the big room. "Here, Bear!" She clapped her hands.

Bear trotted happily across the room to Fern. The line dragged along behind him on the barn's dirt floor.

Lizzie laughed. "He doesn't even seem to notice it."

"That's a good sign," said Fern. "Sometimes puppies get spooked right from the start, and you have to take it very, very slowly." She gave Bear a kiss and a hug. "Now you call him."

Lizzie called, and Bear galloped over. "Yay for Bear!" Lizzie scooped him up for a hug. "What a good puppy." Bear squirmed happily and licked her face.

The girls sent Bear running back and forth a few more times. Then Fern went to the box again and pulled out a chunk of wood, a small log about the size of Lizzie's forearm. "This is the big test." She knelt down and tied the wood to the end of the rope attached to Bear's harness. "Hold him for a sec." She went back to her corner of the room. "Okay, let him go. Here, Bear!"

Bear took off at a gallop. The wood bumpety-bumped along behind him. He stopped for a second and turned to look at it.

What's that *doing there? Oh, well.*

Then he kept going, dashing across to Fern with the log bump-bump-bumping away. When he reached her, he stopped only long enough for a kiss from Fern before he turned around and ran right back to Lizzie, wearing a big doggy grin.

This is great! This is what I was meant to do. I love to pull.

Fern threw up her hands. "Awesome! Lizzie, you were so right."

The barn door slid open. "What's going *on* in here?" Tim Carter stood with his hands on his hips.

"Dad, look! Bear loves to pull." Fern pointed. "Please, can we keep him?"

Tim shook his head. "Honey, I thought I made myself clear. Even if this pup pulled like Balto, I just don't have time to train a puppy right now."

Fern's face fell.

Lizzie felt as if she'd been punched in the stomach.

"I'm sorry, girls." Tim spoke more gently. "I'm sure he'll find a good home with someone who's looking for a pet." Then he put on a smile and clapped his hands. "Hey, how about a ride? I'm about to hitch up my team to the tandem sled. Maybe Lizzie would like to try driving them."

Lizzie knew he was just trying to cheer them up by changing the subject. But she couldn't help herself. "Really?" she asked. "I would love that!"

CHAPTER TEN

"What a racket." Mom had her hands over her ears. It was the next day, and Lizzie was back at Fern and Tim Carter's — along with the rest of her family. It was time for their sled ride.

Tim and Fern were ready for them. Fern had harnessed her team of dogs and hitched them up to her sled. The dogs were so excited. They could not wait to run. Lizzie could hardly believe how loudly they were barking. It sounded like six *hundred* dogs instead of six. Tongues hung out, tails wagged, ears were on high alert. The dogs pawed at the ground and lunged at their lines. It took both Tim and Fern to hold them so that they would not take off by themselves.

After Lizzie put Bear into the puppy pen, she helped Mom into the sled, then settled the Bean on her lap. "You are not going to believe how fun this is." She tucked a blanket around them.

"What about you?" Mom asked.

"We'll be right behind you," Lizzie said. "I'm going to help Tim hitch up his dogs."

Fern climbed onto the runners on the back of her sled, and the dogs went crazy with barking. "Hike!" said Fern. Tim let go of Sitka's harness, and they were off. The dogs stopped barking the instant they began to run. They took off, dashing like lightning across the snowy field.

"Wheee!" Lizzie heard the Bean cry. Lizzie laughed. She could just imagine Mom's face.

"Okay, Lizzie. Let's get our team ready." Tim went to the gate of the pen, grabbed two eager dogs by their collars, and turned them over to Lizzie, who let them drag her over to the sled where the gang line and tug lines were laid out, ready for the dogs to be clipped in. She attached Tater and Spud to the lines nearest the sled. They were the wheel dogs, the ones who helped steer the sled around corners. Tim brought out two more dogs — Donut and Waffle — and clipped them in front of Tater and Spud. Donut and Waffle were the point dogs, the strong ones who helped power the sled. The dogs were raring to go, just like Fern's team. "Maybe you could help hold them!" Tim shouted to Charles and Dad over the wild barking.

Dad stepped forward and grabbed Spud's harness. "Got him!" Charles grabbed Tater's. Tim was already bringing the last two dogs over to get clipped in. Muffin and T-Bone were the lead dogs, strong and bold. They were well trained to pay attention to Tim's commands, but also smart and confident enough to do what they knew was right in any situation. Watching Tim clip them in, Lizzie thought Bear could have been a lead dog someday, if he'd only had the chance.

Tim held T-Bone's harness. "Okay," he shouted. "Lizzie, help your dad and brother into the sled."

"What about you?" Dad looked up at Lizzie as she tucked a blanket around him and Charles. "Where are you riding?"

Lizzie smiled and pointed to the back of the sled. It was Tim's tandem sled, the one she'd been on yesterday, when she'd had the time of her life helping to drive a dog team. "I'm driving!" She headed back to stand on the runners. Her brother and father craned their necks around to stare at her. Charles's mouth fell open.

Lizzie cracked up. "Don't worry! Tim's in charge. But I'll be your copilot."

"She almost *could* drive alone, if she wanted to." Tim yelled over the barking as he took his place behind Lizzie. "She's a natural."

Lizzie beamed. It was true. Driving a team of sled dogs seemed like the most natural thing in the world. It was just like Aunt Amanda had said: If you found the thing that was right for you, you knew it. The day before, driving a sled for the very first time, Lizzie had felt sure of herself right from the start. Somehow she had known just how to lean her weight to one side or another, how to put a foot down to help push the sled like a scooter when the dogs were working hard going up a steep hill, how to know just when to call out "Gee" or "Haw" to get the dogs turning to the right or left when a fork appeared in the trail.

Mushing was the most fun Lizzie had ever had. She was already having Iditarod dreams. Maybe she would adopt Bear and train him to pull her on a scooter. That's how some mushers started, according to Tim. And someday she would have a whole team of dogs. Maybe someday she would win that most amazing race — or even just finish it, which would be enough.

"Okay, Muffin," yelled Tim. "Hike!" And the dogs stopped barking and took off, jerking the sled hard. Silently, the dogs raced up the trail. Swish, swish went the runners of the sled. Jingle, jingle went the dogs' collar tags. The white snow lay deep and soft all around as the team pulled together, working as one with their drivers.

Lizzie's heart was so full, she thought it might burst.

An hour later, back at the Carters' place, everyone sat down for dinner: big bowls of chili that had simmered on the woodstove, homemade bread, and a huge salad.

Charles could not stop talking about the sled ride. Mom and Dad kept telling Lizzie how proud they were of her. And the Bean was so excited, he could hardly eat.

"Cheers!" Tim held up his glass of cider. "Here's to Lizzie, the newest musher on the block."

"Cheers!" said everyone.

Fern clinked glasses with Lizzie. "We have something else to celebrate, too," she announced.

Her eyes sparkled. "Guess what? Dad changed his mind. He decided he was wrong about Bear, once he saw the way he pulled that log. He thought about it overnight and this morning he told me I can adopt Bear, if I promise to do all his training and chip in for his food." She bent to kiss Bear, who dozed on her lap. He opened one eye and licked her hand.

I love my new home. It's cozy and warm inside, and I also get to run and pull things. What could be better?

For just one second, Lizzie felt her heart sink. She had been imagining Bear as *her* dog. But then she smiled. This was so much better. Bear belonged up here in the north, where he would have snow to roll in all winter long and older dogs to teach him the ways of running as a team. She held up her glass. "Congratulations! I think you guys are the *perfect* forever family for Bear."

As they clinked glasses, an eerie noise rose from outside. A howling, yipping, crooning hullabaloo. "What is *that*?" Mom's eyes widened.

"The dogs are singing." Tim got up to open the door. "They do it all the time. One starts and the others join in. Sometimes we sing along with them." He poked his head outside. "I think I know why they started. Come see!"

Everybody jumped up from the table and ran to the door. Tim pointed straight overhead. Lizzie looked up to see brilliant streaks of red and green pulsing across the sky, filling the darkness with dancing veils of color. "Oh!" She drew in a breath of clear, cold air. "How beautiful!"

"It's the northern lights," Fern whispered. "The whole sky is celebrating with us!"

And Bear, nestled in her arms, lifted up his little nose to the sky and joined in the howling chorus.

PUPPY TIPS

Sled-dog racing is a very exciting sport. But did you know that sled dogs have been used in other ways? Long ago, sled-dog teams helped explorers discover new parts of the world, in the Arctic and in Antarctica (sled dogs are no longer allowed in Antarctica, because of that continent's fragile ecology). And sled dogs are still used today for transportation and hunting in many northern places where there are no roads.

A dog does not have to be a husky to want to pull. You probably know that from walking your dog on a leash! Almost any dog can be a sled dog if it is trained right. Believe it or not, a team of *poodles* ran the Iditarod four times. They finished the race each time and even did pretty well!

Dear Reader,

Guess what I did one day last winter? I went for a dogsled ride! Before the ride, I got to hang out with the dogs and get to know them a little. Then I got to help harness them. When we hooked them up to the sled, they were so excited, they were jumping up and down and barking their heads off. And when they started pulling, watch out! We took off like a race car.

One great thing about being a writer is that you get to do research. To make sure I'm getting things right, when I write the Puppy Place books I like to check things out for myself. I have visited stables, dog groomers, firehouses, animal shelters, and doggy day-care centers. I've talked to all kinds of people and learned all kinds of interesting things. But the dogsled ride was my favorite research project ever.

Yours from the Puppy Place,
Ellen Miles

ABOUT THE AUTHOR

Ellen Miles likes to write about the different personalities of dogs. She is the author of more than 28 books, including the Puppy Place and Taylor-Made Tales series as well as *The Pied Piper* and other Scholastic Classics. Ellen loves to be outdoors every day, walking, biking, skiing, or swimming, depending on the season. She also loves to read, cook, explore her beautiful state, and hang out with friends and family. She lives in Vermont.

If you love animals, be sure to read all the adorable stories in the Puppy Place series!